Dennis Clayfield Ireland

Pros and Cons of Leasehold Enfranchisement

Dennis Clayfield Ireland

Pros and Cons of Leasehold Enfranchisement

ISBN/EAN: 9783337403003

Printed in Europe, USA, Canada, Australia, Japan

Cover: Foto ©Andreas Hilbeck / pixelio.de

More available books at **www.hansebooks.com**

PROS AND CONS

OF

LEASEHOLD

ENFRANCHISEMENT.

BY

DENNIS CLAYFIELD, IRELAND.

———••••———

CASSELL & COMPANY, Limited:

LONDON, PARIS, NEW YORK & MELBOURNE.

1888.

NOTE.

—◆—

In the following pages I have tried to indicate briefly the general line and drift of the evidence given before the Town Holdings Committee with regard to Leasehold Enfranchisement. It is hardly necessary for me to observe that, so far as the arguments used on either side are concerned, I can lay no claim to originality of any kind. So many books and pamphlets on this subject have already been published that it would now be extremely difficult to say anything about it which should be at once new and true. But as the facts and figures here set forth are derived to a great extent from the recently published Blue Book, I venture to hope that this pamphlet may be of some service to local politicians, candidates for urban constituencies, and other unfortunate people whose duty it may be to make themselves acquainted with the latest information on all the political questions of the day.

D. C. I.

9 Old Square, Lincoln's Inn,
December 1888.

PROS AND CONS

OF

LEASEHOLD ENFRANCHISEMENT.

—◆✕◆—

I.

THE main facts in the history of the agitation for Lease
hold Enfranchisement are few and fairly simple. According
to the *Daily News*, the movement was at the outset based
in great measure on æsthetic considerations. "The ugly,
lamentable effects of the leasehold system upon domestic
architecture, and the ugly and lamentable effects of that
architecture upon the tastes and the character of dwellers
in 'brick-boxes'—that, rather than the fiscal and other
material injustices of the leasehold system, was what chiefly
arrested the attention of *Review* writers on the question
sixteen years ago. When, a dozen years later, the politicians and publicists took the question up systematically,
they soon discovered they were labouring upon a soil fully
prepared." Foremost among the fortunate persons here
referred to stood Mr. Henry Broadhurst, who was then
member for Stoke, Mr. James Rowlands, who is now
member for Finsbury, and Mr. Howard Evans, the author
of "Our Old Nobility" and other useful works. These
three gentlemen some four years ago founded the Leaseholds Enfranchisement Association, of which the first-
named is past-President, the second is Secretary, and the
last is Honorary Secretary. The object of this Associa-

tion is, says Mr. Evans, " to obtain for urban leaseholders compulsory power of purchasing the fee simple on equitable terms ; or, to put the matter still more simply, to enable a man who holds the lease of a house to buy up the ground-rent." The Association seems to have thriven and grown rapidly. Before the end of the first year of its existence (1884) nearly forty members of Parliament had joined it, and more than a hundred thousand copies of publications on the leasehold question had been distributed by its agency throughout London and the provinces. Nor was this enthusiasm destined soon to spend itself. At the Association's third annual meeting, which was attended by a crofter from Glendale and by a Queen's Counsel from Lincoln's Inn, the chairman " was much pleased to be able to say that the Association was gathering strength every day. The members had every reason to congratulate themselves on the increased amount of support that was now being given to the programme of the Association ; in fact, the public interest evinced in it was so great and so earnest that it would be very difficult for a Liberal candidate in an urban constituency where the leasehold system prevailed to abjure them or the work they were seeking to do. So far from that being the case, the tendency of such candidates was to make the objects of the Association more and more a main plank in their platform." And at this year's meeting the same chairman was able to announce, amid loud and prolonged applause, that " during the last year the Enfranchisement movement had received the support of the leaders of the Liberal party, and particularly of the leader of its leaders, Mr. Gladstone."

So much for the progress of the movement hitherto throughout the constituencies. Within the House of Commons the zeal and activity of the chief supporters of Leasehold Enfranchisement have been no less conspicuous, and date from a time when the Association itself had not come into existence. Every year since 1882 at least one Bill dealing with the matter has been brought in ; in one year two Bills were brought in, in another year three Bills. Most of these Bills—which have been altered greatly from year to year—have borne the name of Mr. Broadhurst, the first President of the Association, or of Mr. H. L. W. Lawson, the present President. Two of them, however, were of a less official stamp, and though both have long since been dropped, they possess some historical importance as having been introduced, one by a learned and gallant Conservative member, and the other by Lord Randolph Churchill. But Mr. Lawson's Leaseholders (Purchase of Fee Simple) Bill is the only one which is now before Parliament or with which we need concern ourselves at present.

"The object of this Bill," as we are told in a Memorandum prefixed to it, " is to carry out the recommendation of the Royal Commission on the Housing of the Working Classes in their Supplementary Report, viz.:—' That legislation favourable to the acquisition, on equitable terms, of the freehold interest on the part of the leaseholder would conduce greatly to the improvement of the dwellings of the people of this country,' on the ground ' that the prevailing system of building-leases is conducive to bad building, to deterioration of property towards the close of the lease, and to a want of interest on the part of the occupier in the house he inhabits,' and that ' the system of building on leasehold land is a great cause of the many evils connected with overcrowding, unsanitary buildings, and excessive rents.' "

Now before we proceed to examine in greater or less detail the various charges which these Commissioners brought against the building-lease system, it may be well to point out one remarkable circumstance in connection with their Supplementary Report. It has been shown more than once that this Report, from which Lord Salisbury expressly dissented and in which some of the most eminent members of the Commission—Sir Charles Dilke, Mr. Goschen, Lord Cross, and the then Bishop of Bedford—did not join, whether justified or not by the facts of the case, was certainly not justified by the evidence which had been given before the Commission. That evidence was no doubt directed to the evils caused by overcrowding, unsanitary buildings, and excessive rents. But from the beginning to the end of it no attempt was made to prove that the evils in question were attributable to one building system rather than another, and, as a matter of fact, some of the worst cases of overcrowding, etc., mentioned in the Commissioners' principal Report occurred on freehold land. It is obvious, therefore, that these *obiter dicta* of Cardinal Manning, Lord Carrington, and the rest, though worthy of all respect and consideration, do not form a very solid basis on which to found a drastic and far-reaching reform.

That this was the general opinion among men of all parties seems indeed tolerably clear from the course which events subsequently took. Within a twelvemonth after the publication of the Report of the Royal Commission, a debate arose in the House of Commons on an Irish Member's Bill for giving compensation for improvements to urban occupiers, and Mr. Gladstone's Government thereupon consented to the appointment of a Select Committee of the House to inquire into " the terms of occupation and the compensation for improvements possessed by the occupiers of town houses and holdings in Great Britain and Ireland ; " and when the Committee were formally nominated a few weeks later, they were further directed to inquire into " the expediency of giving to leaseholders facilities for the purchase of the fee simple of their property." On the dissolution of Parliament in June 1886 the work of the Town Holdings Committee was brought to an abrupt end ; but the ten thousand questions and answers (relating principally to Ireland) to which they had devoted their fourteen sittings were reported in a Blue Book, and their recommendation that another Committee, with the same objects, should be appointed in the approaching Parliament was adopted at the beginning of 1887. The new Committee, which took evidence on twenty-eight days from February to August, reported that evidence to the House in a second Blue Book of over eight hundred pages, and similarly recommended that a Committee on the same subject should be appointed in the next Session of Parliament. In February of this year the Select Committee were accordingly re-appointed, and they took further evidence at thirty-one sittings. On the 31st of last July they reported this evidence in a third Blue Book, and, while desiring to take further evidence on another branch of their inquiry, they expressed a hope that it may not be necessary for them to call further witnesses as to the expediency of giving to leaseholders facilities for the purchase of the fee simple of their property. With regard to Leasehold Enfranchisement, therefore, it would seem probable that we are now in possession of all the evidence on which the final Report of the Town Holdings Committee will be based, and we can at last decide how far the charges brought against the leasehold system by Mr. Broadhurst and his Association friends, and by Cardinal Manning and the nine other Royal Commissioners, have been substantiated by the opponents of that system or rebutted by its supporters.

II.

THE first charge brought by the Royal Commissioners
against " the prevailing system of building-leases " — by
which we must understand the ordinary London lease of
ninety-nine years or thereabouts—was that it led to bad
building. This charge was repeated in general terms by
several of the earlier witnesses called before the Town
Holdings Committee. Mr. Charles Harrison, " the eminent
London solicitor " (as his Association friends love to style
him), said that his practical experience would certainly tend
to confirm the Supplementary Report. Mr. Stockall, a Past
Grand Master of the Manchester Unity of Oddfellows, said
that in his opinion there was " a tendency " to build worse
houses on leasehold than on freehold land. And Mr. Burr,
of the Landed Estates Agency, Limited, said that a better
class of house would be built on a freehold than on a ninety-
nine years' term. On the other hand there was an over-
whelming mass of evidence to show that differences of
tenure have little or nothing to do with the quality of buildings. Thus—to confine ourselves to the testimony of dis
interested or hostile witnesses—Mr. Yates, a builder who
gave evidence against the leasehold system, said that he
would make no difference at all in the class of building he
put upon freehold and leasehold land ; one house would be
a *fac-simile* of the other. Mr. Brevitt, the town clerk of
Wolverhampton, who gave evidence somewhat in favour of
the freehold system, being asked whether the tenure of the
land had much effect upon the character of the buildings
on it, said, " We do not find it so in Wolverhampton." Mr.
Clark, the secretary of the Leaseholds Enfranchisement
Association in Devonport, asked by Mr. Rowlands what he
thought was the effect of the leasehold system upon the
classes of house, answered that he did not think there was

much to choose between a freehold and a leasehold. Mr. Wallis, the Duke of Devonshire's Eastbourne agent, though he expressed a decided preference for freehold houses, said that " if a speculative builder can get hold of a piece of ground, and buy the fee out and out, and is allowed to run his course, he certainly will not put up anything better than he is obliged to ; " he will only satisfy the public requirements, which are less stringent and effective than those of a lessor's surveyor would be. Mr. Josiah Thomas, city surveyor at Bristol, who gave evidence in support of the fee-farm system prevalent in that dirty and dilapidated city, said that, comparing the land let upon the ninety-nine years' system with land let upon the freehold perpetual ground-rent system, the character of the buildings, as regarded their substantialness and otherwise, so far as his experience went, did not differ upon the two systems. Many other trustworthy witnesses gave evidence to the same effect.

But though the question of freehold or leasehold tenure seems thus to be immaterial with regard to the original quality of a house, the Royal Commissioners may nevertheless have been right in supposing that the leasehold system is conducive " to deterioration of property towards the close of the lease, and to a want of interest on the part of the occupier in the house he inhabits." How, then, does the evidence stand in respect of this second charge ? On the one hand Mr. Rhodes, of Beckenham, a member of the Leaseholds Enfranchisement Association, said, in reference to industrial property, that he would expect great advantages from the power of a lessee to enfranchise, because there would be the avoidance of the notorious " fag end of lease " proceedings. The evil, in his opinion, resided in the dual ownership, which must be a greater mischief at the end of a lease than during its currency. Mr. Harrison said the opinion he had formed was that the class of property built was worse on leasehold than on free-hold, notably from the fact of there being no fag end of leases or terms on freeholds as on leaseholds which allowed of property being rack-rented. He added that there are certain men who carry on a kind of business in purchasing fag ends of leases at a comparatively small price, and that these men could not live under a freehold system. And Mr. Benjamin Jones, the Honorary Secretary of the Parliamentary Committee of the Co-operative Union, said that he had seen some London houses and working-class dwellings at the fag end of leases, and that these were in his opinion wretched, it being nobody's interest to repair them if they could possibly help it, only so far as the ground landlord compelled them. On the other hand a number of witnesses gave evidence to the effect that the ground landlord had an unpleasant habit of compelling his lessees to repair. Thus, Mr. Cooper, a builder residing at Beckenham, complained somewhat bitterly of the dictation and interference by freeholders in the matter of repairs and in the enforcement of restrictive covenants. And Mr. Holmes, who came as a representative man from the Friendly Societies of London, while he alleged that a large number of lessees purposely neglected to keep their houses in repair, especially if they were men of no position, and that there were a number of people of no stability what-ever who purchased fag ends of leases for the purpose of making as much as they could out of them, at the same time expressed his conviction that, if it were possible for a lessee to buy the absolute fee simple of his house, it would save a lot of bother and interference on the part of the freeholder. And even where such interference has not been exercised and a house has consequently been suffered to fall into a state of disrepair, there would seem to be more hope for it on the leasehold than on the freehold system. Mr. Yates, whose evidence has already been referred to,

said that in the case of worn-out property at the end of a
lease the best thing the freeholder can possibly do is to
pull it down or rebuild it, and that that was really about
the history of a great deal of such property. According to
Mr. Green, a working man employed at Woolwich Arsenal
and an ardent advocate of Leasehold Enfranchisement,
leases are usually forfeited three or four years before the
end of them, and the ground landlord takes them over in
whatever condition they may be in. Under the leasehold
system, said Mr. Vigers, the surveyor to the Peabody Trustees, there is an end to dilapidations when the lease falls
in ; the freeholder then comes into possession, and is able
to deal with the property and get rid of those pest-places.
Under the freehold system the dilapidations go on until
the Board of Works, or some other local authority, steps in
and clears the district at an enormous cost to the ratepayers.

As to the rather vague charge which the Royal Commissioners brought next — namely, that the system of
building-leases is conducive to "a want of interest on the
part of the occupier in the house he inhabits"—it is perhaps
enough to say that the great bulk of occupiers are not and
never will be lessees, but hold on weekly or monthly
tenancies, and it makes no difference whatever to them
whether the persons to whom they pay rent are freeholders
or not. In the comparatively small class of occupying
owners occupying leaseholders are, it is said, more numerous
in proportion to the entire body of leaseholders than occupying freeholders are in proportion to the entire body of freeholders. That thrifty working men feel at any rate no sort
of abhorrence of leasehold houses and do not hesitate to
invest their savings in them, is abundantly proved by the
evidence of several well-informed witnesses. Thus, Mr.
Stockall—who, though he will not pledge himself to the
details of Mr. Lawson's Bill, is in favour of the principle of

Leasehold Enfranchisement—said that the leasehold system, in his opinion, rather stimulated the desire of the working classes to acquire their houses. What working men liked was seven or eight per cent. interest. Some years ago he himself belonged to a building society, and he was fortunate enough to draw a ballot and had £300 lent him free of interest. With this money he purchased a small leasehold house. In ten years he paid the whole sum back, and he then sold the house for £100 more than he had given for it. This, he said, could not possibly have happened if the house had been freehold. And though two or more Welsh witnesses bore testimony to the strong desire among the quarrymen to build their own houses, and said that building societies would, it was believed, charge a lower rate of interest for loans on freehold than on leasehold property, some exceedingly strong evidence to the contrary was given by Mr. Wintringham, of Great Grimsby, the solicitor and agent of Mr. Heneage. This gentleman, who declared himself in favour of Leasehold Enfranchisement provided that the restrictive covenants could be maintained and fair terms were given to the freeholders, said that since 1860 there have been built 989 houses on Mr. Heneage's estate. Of these about 350 are working men's houses with under £12 a year rent. The leases are for ninety-nine years, and the ground-rent is twopence a square yard. The working men's houses have been built by companies formed of working men themselves, and now most of them occupy the houses themselves. Out of the 989 houses, 223 are occupied by the actual lessees. In 1884 Mr. Heneage sent out a letter offering to enfranchise any part of his property on twenty-five years' purchase of the ground-rent; but though the offer was considered a fair one, only thirty-two out of the holders of 989 leases applied. And yet, as Mr. Wintringham said, "when the building societies on Mr. Heneage's estate had cleared off their mortgages, they might have gone on a little bit longer contributing amongst themselves, and have bought the ground-rent and made the property freehold before they divided, but there is not one of them that has done that. They have kept it leasehold. We have on Mr. Heneage's estate perhaps a dozen of these societies, who have built their houses by contributions amongst themselves and borrowing. They have gone on contributing and then have paid off their mortgages, and have conveyed to each man his house, leasehold, whereas by remaining a few years longer they could have formed a fund and bought out the ground-rent and bought the freehold; but, as I say, they have none of them considered it worth while to do so." In Wolverhampton, on the other hand, where house property is held almost exclusively upon freehold tenure, there are from 1,500 to 2,000 property owners, and a year ago there were 16,607 houses; so that, although the freehold system has always prevailed there, at least seven-eighths of the occupiers have abstained from purchasing their houses. Mr. Brevitt, who gave evidence on this point, thought indeed that where a working man is in a position to acquire property he would rather it was on freehold than on lease-hold tenure; but he expressed a hope that he had not "conveyed an impression to this effect upon the mind of the Committee, that the working men of Wolverhampton are anxious to become freeholders." And, apart from working men, there is ample and unquestionable evidence that lessees in general do not care to buy the freeholds subject to their leases. Mr. Edward Tewson, whose experience in this matter is perhaps unrivalled, said : " I have examined the books of my firm for the past ten years. I have taken out from those, because I do not think it is quite fair to intro-duce them in any inquiry like this, all the large ground-rents, those representing £200, £300, £500, or £1,000 a year, and I find that we have sold 182 ground-rents in the public market by auction ; of course, thrown open to everybody ;

the outside public and the lessee have all had notice of the sales, and I have found out of those 182 only 24 of the lessees have purchased their freehold properties." And not only do lessees seldom care to acquire " on equitable terms " the freehold interest in their holdings, but several instances were given to the Committee of a common desire among freeholders to become lessees. Mr. Vigers said he thought it an advantage to the trading classes to be able to get building-leases (which, by the way, Mr. Harrison " certainly would prohibit in future ") rather than to be forced to buy the freehold. " A man carrying on business," said he, " in my experience, you never find very much overburdened with capital. He cannot afford to invest his money in his freehold, and get only four or five per cent., when, if he brings his money into his business, he can make eight or ten per cent. ; and, practically, I can give examples of where men have been the freeholders of their land, built their trade establishments, and then sold the freehold ground-rent upon which it is built. I have two now for sale, where the man, being the freeholder of the land, spent very large sums of money in putting up his trade premises, and then he finds it better for him to get the money back into his business rather than to remain the freeholder. He sells the freehold right out, and then takes a lease for eighty years." And later on in his evidence Mr. Vigers referred to the case of the Holborn Viaduct, where " the people who put up the buildings bought the freehold, but since then they have all been transferred into leaseholds, and the Crown has bought up the ground-rents. Leases have been granted at fixed rents, and the Crown has bought those ground-rents ; so that every man who had the opportunity there, or the men who deal with the whole of that estate, had the opportunity of being freeholders, but it paid them better to sell their freeholds and turn them into leaseholds." Mr. Tewson said he had known numerous cases where owners of freehold land or trade premises had converted themselves into lessees for ninety-nine years, and he had known also, and had been concerned in, a great many cases in which an occupying freeholder had sold his property out and out, and had then become a lessee at a rack-rent, at a percentage upon the price realised. Mortgages, as he said, were liable to be called in, whereas the leases created could not be called in, and the lessee would not be required to pay the money back. And Mr. Garrard, the surveyor, said he had known many persons who wished to cover a site with a building come to him and say, " When I have put this building up, will you buy that ground-rent of me when it is secured ? "— thus making themselves leaseholders to enable them to build and to make a profit. Whatever, therefore, the Royal Commissioners may have meant by ascribing to the system of building-leases " a want of interest on the part of the occupier in the house he inhabits," there can be no sort of doubt that occupiers who are able and willing to own their houses are not deterred from buying them because they are only leasehold, and that in many cases it pays such occupiers to remain leaseholders rather than to become freeholders, or even to become leaseholders rather than to remain freeholders.

Let us now pass on to consider whether the Commissioners were right in their view that " the system of building on leasehold land is a great cause of the many evils connected with overcrowding, unsanitary buildings, and excessive rents." These evils were, of course, the very things which the Commissioners had been appointed to inquire into, and it will be remembered that at the time of their appointment a great and almost hysterical interest was taken in the subject by the general public and by many fashionable persons. With regard to overcrowding, however, little evidence was given before the Town Holdings Committee, and such as was given does not help either side very much. The upshot of it seems to be that here again tenure makes hardly any difference. Mr. Howard Martin, a London surveyor and land agent, said that some of the worst over-crowding is found in the freehold houses; the sanitary authorities, not the ground landlords, are the proper people to prevent it. It would, in his opinion, be a most injurious interference with the liberty of the leaseholder that a ground landlord should have the power to dictate how many people should live in a house when it was built. Mr. Boodle, the solicitor and agent of the Duke of West-minster, Lord Northampton, and others, said that he thought there was more overcrowding in small freeholds than on large estates; on small freehold estates there were more of the poorer classes living in single rooms than upon the estates of large owners. This evidence is perhaps a trifle vague. Yet on the whole Mr. Boodle was probably not far wrong when he said that "if a man hardens his heart, and treats his fellow-creatures like brute beasts, and crowds them in like pigs, this system of farming houses is the most remunerative thing possible. . . . It is a thing that land-lords do their best to check; but I think it would im-mensely increase under the facilities for acquiring separate freeholds."

Unsanitary buildings are, of course, closely connected with overcrowding, and it would appear that the building-lease system has no more to do with the former than with the latter. Mr. Brevitt, who, as has already been men-tioned, rather advocates the freehold system, gave the Committee some interesting information respecting a "con-demned area" in Wolverhampton which some time ago was acquired by the Corporation under the Artizans Dwellings Acts. The whole, or practically the whole, of this area was held on freehold tenure. "In that area there were 46 new houses. Medium and in good repair, 118 ; old and in good order, 78; old and dilapidated, 408. In ruins and condemned as unfit for human habitation, 54 ; and out of a total number of 704 houses in the area only 113 had ample area in accordance with the requirements of our local Act ; houses with insufficient area, 591." "The sanitary defects," Mr. Brevitt added, " were such as to be irremediable except by some improvement scheme which would lead to the demolition of most of the houses with a view to a re-arrangement of dwellings and a reconstruction of streets within the area. Much of the property was totally unfit for human habitation, and so dilapidated as to become mere receptacles of offal and filth, giving rise to dangers of the most serious nature to the sanitary well-being of the borough." Mr. Martin said he thought that the existence of a landlord who would enforce the repairing covenants was a good thing for the occupiers. " If," he said, " the tenure makes any difference at all, it makes a difference in that direction ; and in very many instances I found it had made that difference." And in the course of his evidence he referred to a large block of property between Catherine-street, Russell-street, and Drury-lane, east and west, and the Strand and Long-acre, north and south. The southern part of it lies off the Bedford estate, and a con-siderable part of it is freehold. " A very bad part of it,' said Mr. Martin, " is New Church-court. That is a place that was found to be in a most deplorable condition, so bad, in fact, that a large part of it has been shut up by the sani-tary authorities, so I am told. At any rate, the houses have been closed recently, since I first saw them. Of those houses most are freehold, some two or three are small lease-holds. Then there is Feathers-court, which is another court close by. Just north of these there are a great many courts —Duke's-court, Cross-court, Crown-court, Martlett's-court, and there are a great many other courts on the Bedford estate,

B

and there is no apparent reason whatever why they should not be as bad as the courts I have just mentioned, except that they have been under the control of the ground landlord's agents and surveyors. It is a particularly good case in point, because in Martlett's-court, curiously enough, there are four freeholds which happen to be in the middle of the leasehold houses, and any one walking down Martlett's-court could pick out those at once, because they are so much worse than the leaseholds adjoining." As an instance of well-managed tenement property Mr. Martin mentioned Albion-place, which is at the south-east corner of Clerkenwell. This is leasehold property, with thirty years unexpired, and stands, as he said, "in a particularly disadvantageous position and surrounded by exceedingly bad property, and therefore situated in a district where it is difficult to get the best kind of tenants. Notwithstanding that, the whole of that Albion-place property is in a most excellent condition, and it is occupied by respectable tenants. The place itself, though a narrow one, is kept clean, and the houses are kept in good order. There is an instance of the superiority of the leasehold system." Mr. Martin said he did not know who the ground landlord of this property was; it was a small leasehold, not on one of the large estates. To his evidence, the importance and suggestiveness of which are manifest, may be added that of Mr. Forwood, the Secretary to the Admiralty, who said that so far as sound buildings and convenience for the public streets and sanitary and other purposes are concerned, the houses in Liverpool built upon leasehold land are, he thinks, better than those built upon freehold land.

But though it seems hardly to have been argued before the Town Holdings Committee that the many evils connected with overcrowded and unsanitary buildings are due to the building-lease system, the theory that this system is responsible for "excessive rents" found favour with several of the witnesses. Mr. Rhodes, for example, said that the rents of industrial property must obviously be made higher by the fact that a sinking fund has to be provided in order to replace the lessee's capital. Mr. Cooper, the Beckenham builder, said that whereas he had to pay five per cent. for loans on leasehold land, he could borrow at four per cent. on freeholds ; and being asked who really paid the difference between the four and the five per cent.—whether it was the builder, or the person to whom he let the house— he answered, " Of course I charge higher rent, because I have to pay more interest." And Mr. Yates, with reference to some property near London which he was developing on the freehold system, said that he could borrow capital on it at a lower rate of interest than on leasehold, and was able to let that property ten or twelve per cent. cheaper than he could have done if there had been two ownerships. He admitted, however, that if the property had been leasehold he could not have obtained ten per cent. more from the tenants, but would have been prevented from developing the land. Now it seems clear that, as Mr. Garrard said, the rent ultimately paid by the occupier is not directly affected by the question of tenure at all. A working man, or any other man, will not pay a higher rent for a house because his landlord has to provide a sinking fund or has had to borrow on the house at five per cent. If Thomas Smith gets No. 1 for six shillings a week, then, sinking fund or no sinking fund, John Jones will not pay a penny more for No. 2. But, indeed, there is positive evidence that on the whole the leasehold system tends indirectly to make houses cheaper both for owners and for occupiers. Thus Mr. Spain, who manages three building estates for Lord and Lady Northbourne—the land on two of them being let on ninety-nine years' leases, and on the third being sold out and out to the builders—said that from his practical acquaintance with both systems he considered that the houses under the leasehold system were acquired at a cheaper rate than under the freehold, and that this might be accounted for by the fact that leasehold land was let at a ground-rent the capitalised value of which was low when compared with the price paid for the freehold. Mr. Simpson, a solicitor practising in Sheffield, who is "entirely in favour of the power being given to a lessee to enfranchise leaseholds," objects to the leasehold system mainly on the ground that it "encourages a larger amount of building" than the free-hold system, and therefore a town where the leasehold system prevails is more likely to be over-built than a town where the freehold system prevails. "Supposing," said Mr. Simpson, "in Sheffield land could only be obtained by persons acquiring the fee simple, I do not think there would be anything like the buildings in the town that there are now." The chairman, Mr. Lewis Fry, thereupon asked him :

"Do you think the towns, as a whole, and the popula-tion, would benefit by the change, or the reverse ?—The occupiers would benefit.

"They would have to pay higher rents, would they not ? —They get houses at lower rents when there are many houses.

"Under the leasehold system ?—Yes, no doubt. It is beneficial, I am sure, to the occupier, because there are more houses than tenants.

"You mean the leasehold system in that way is bene-ficial to the occupiers ?—Yes, it is.

"But I understand you to intimate that you think the character of the houses built is rather inferior?—Yes, I think the leasehold houses are rather inferior.

"Freehold houses would cost more, and in that way the rent would have to be more, I suppose ?—Yes, it would have to be more ; there is no doubt about that."

And Mr. William Mathews, of Birmingham, one of the

best-known land agents and surveyors in the Midlands,
after remarking that there were plenty of "jerry-builders"
and "land jobbers" in that town, and that—though he
does not think there is "the slightest difference in the
quality of working men's houses built upon leasehold or
freehold"—these builders and jobbers operated entirely
upon leasehold land, went on to say that the leasehold
system "encourages the building of a great number of
small houses, and the fact of building a large number of
small houses by increasing the supply has a tendency to
decrease the rents." If builders of this description were
excluded from the market, "the permanence of the houses
might be improved," but "certainly rents would be raised
by it. . . . I think the poorer class of occupiers as
a class are benefited by the most rapid production of
the commodity which they require."

III.

WE have now inquired one by one into the various charges
which the Royal Commissioners brought against the prevailing system of building-leases, and have found that none
of these charges has been proved, and that most if not
all of them have been distinctly disproved, by the witnesses who gave evidence, on one side or the other, before
the Town Holdings Committee. It remains for us to see
how Mr. Lawson proposes to carry out the recommendation
which the Royal Commissioners based on these unjust
charges, how far his Bill itself is just, and who are likely
to be benefited and who to be injured by this or any other
scheme of Leasehold Enfranchisement.

Now the recommendation of the Commissioners, it will
be remembered, was "that legislation favourable to the

acquisition, on equitable terms, of the freehold interest on
the part of the leaseholder would conduce greatly to the improvement of the dwellings of the people of this country ";
and the Memorandum which is prefixed to the Bill, and
which has been already referred to, states generally the
method by which this end is to be attained. " The Bill,"
we are told, " affects all leases having a term of twenty
years unexpired, as well as all leases for lives. Sub-leases
are treated as leases for the purpose of enfranchisement.
The initial process is, on the customary lines, to compel the
lessor or lessors, by notice, to estimate the present value of
their interests, and the lessee, wishing to enfranchise, to
offer a counter-price, with a reference, if they cannot agree,
to the county or other analogous court.*   The capital sum
or sums having been settled by agreement or by the court,
power is given to those who were lessees, or their successors
in title, to substitute a terminable or perpetual rent-charge
for the capital payment, with the consent of the person or
persons who had the reversionary interest. Covenants pro-
viding for restraint on user can be enforced, either by the
original lessor or by the local authority, which can also,
under proper safeguards, release the property from certain
kinds of covenants.   Inquiry into title is regulated by sec-
tion 2, Vendor and Purchaser Act, 1874, whilst the court
has larger powers in cases of doubt or difficulty. Legal
expenses are limited, and a scale of costs is provided." It
may be worth while to add that the Bill applies only to
demised buildings or land not exceeding three acres in extent ; that a lessee is not to be entitled to exercise his right
of enfranchisement in respect of part only of the premises
demised by his lease, except where such part is the subject

---

* Mr. Charles Harrison, whom the *Daily News* describes as "perhaps
the first living authority on the subject" of London leases, in his evidence
before the Town Holdings Committee said that he did not think the county
courts a fit and proper tribunal.

of a separate tenancy; that the purchase-money is to be "the sum which, in the opinion of the court, is the value of the present interests with the reversions in question expectant upon the determination of the lease"; and that "in taxing costs under this Act only one set of costs shall be allowed as payable by the lessee, except in cases where the court shall otherwise order."

The first idea which must occur to everybody on reading and considering this Memorandum to the Bill or the Bill itself is that, rightly or wrongly, the scheme involves a gigantic and unparalleled interference with the principle of freedom of contract. The scope and extent of the measure are indeed almost incalculable. Mr. Mathews told the Committee that the value of the fee simple in possession of the property affected by the Bill is in Birmingham alone twenty-five millions of pounds. And Mr. Statter, a land agent and surveyor practising in Bury and Manchester, said that in twenty-six municipal boroughs in Lancashire the capital value of the property which would be subject to compulsory Leasehold Enfranchisement was a hundred and thirty-four millions. A precedent for such a statutory revolution in the relations of landlord and tenant has, it is true, been found to the satisfaction of some persons in the Acts relating to the enfranchisement of copyholds. Asked by Mr. Lawson whether he considered that the case of copyholds and their enfranchisement was analogous to that of leaseholds, Mr. Harrison answered that he thought there was the strongest analogy between the two systems. "I regard," said he, "for all practical purposes, a term of years created by a lease, whether dependent upon life or for a fixed term, as identical, for the purposes of considering this Bill, with that of a copyhold tenant holding for lives." But, as was afterwards pointed out to him in the course of his examination, though compulsory enfranchisement of copyholds applies where there is perpetuity, copyholds for lives without a right of renewal—which are the only kind of copyholds really analogous to leaseholds—are expressly excepted from the Acts. It is obvious, moreover, that in the case of copyhold enfranchisement no violence is done to any contract ; for, as Mr. Elton said, "the contract is only imaginary, and is lost in the depths of time." In fact, all that copyhold enfranchisement did was to enable either lord or tenant to substitute a convenient for an inconvenient form of tenure, and there was no more interference with freedom of contract in that case than there was when tithes in coin were substituted for tithes in kind.

But the precedent of copyhold enfranchisement was not the only string to Mr. Harrison's bow. Mr. Lawson put to him the following question :—

"As you are aware, there has been a very great deal of vague talk, with reference to Leasehold Enfranchisement, about interference with contract. . . . I dare say you can illustrate, as a lawyer, from your own very great practical knowledge, cases where the law does interfere with this sup-posed freedom of contract at the present time with regard to land ? "

"Yes, certainly," said Mr. Harrison. "First of all, we may take the ordinary case, that of freeholder and tenant working copper furnace works ; they could not carry on their copper furnace works, however much they might like to do so, to the injury of their neighbours."

This is truly a remarkable illustration, with which land-lord and tenant and freedom of contract have no more necessary connection than the Man in the Moon has. Nobody in the world would maintain that the police or the local authority or the High Court ought to be prevented from putting a stop to a public or private nuisance because it happened to be committed in pursuance of some con-tract. Mr. Harrison might as well have argued that it would be an interference with the freedom of contract if A were prevented from killing B when C had promised to pay him a hundred pounds for the job. Several other illustrations—such as contracts by tenants to pay income-tax, a landlord agreeing to let a house at less than its rateable value, assessment not thereby reduced, &c.—were added by Mr. Harrison; but as most of them are irrelevant, and none of them is quite to the point, it seems hardly worth while to discuss them. We may, perhaps, safely conclude that if Mr. Harrison has failed to find a precedent for Leasehold Enfranchisement, no precedent for it can be found.

"Ah, but," say the Enfranchisers, "if it comes to talking about freedom of contract, where is the freedom of contract under the present leasehold system?" Indeed, Mr. Harrison went so far in this direction as to assert that in most parts of the metropolis freedom of contract is "quite a phrase;" and as "a very strong instance" he mentioned the tyranny of Lord Craven's trustees, who insisted on the insertion of a clause in their building-agreements and leases to the effect that the lessees would "deliver up, for and during such time or times as the same may be required for that purpose, the whole or such part or parts of the premises hereby demised as is or are subject or liable to be taken for a pest-house, surgeon's house, burial-ground, or any or either of them, in the event of a plague happening during the term hereby granted." This "very strong instance" does not appear to constitute a particularly substantial sort of grievance. But, in truth, ample and incontrovertible evidence was given to show—what most people would naturally assume to be the case—that freedom of contract is not a mere phrase or anything like it ; that land in this country is not a monopoly ; that the competition between landowners is every bit as keen as it is between builders ; and that even in London there is always plenty of freehold land to be bought by any one who is willing to pay the market price for it. Mr. Harrison

is able, no doubt, to point to many important towns in
the North and the West of England where the system of
building-leases is unknown or unpopular, and he says
this circumstance shows that it is an artificial and unnatural
system, which has been imposed on helpless Londoners
by ecclesiastical and ducal monopolists. But surely such
facts as that Sir John Ramsden found it expedient to
obtain statutory powers enabling him to let his land at
Huddersfield on long terms, or that the Corporation of
Bristol, having tried in vain to let their Portishead estate on
short terms, were obliged to get leave from the Treasury to
grant it in fee, prove how difficult it is for any landowner
to impose on the inhabitants of a place systems or tenures
to which they are not accustomed. As Mr. Thomas, of
Bristol, said, " In every town in England you find a
different state of things exists. . . . It is possible to
make a general law, but if there was any alteration in the
law, whatever the alteration was, the people in some
localities would have to be educated up to it." The reason
why in London, Birmingham, and other large towns comparatively short terms are prevalent is that the land there
has, from an early date in the history of the development
of those towns, commanded a very high price, and some
system of hiring sites instead of buying them has become
essential for the cheap production of houses. " In towns,"
said Mr. John Morley in the course of the debate which
resulted in the appointment of the first Town Holdings
Committee, " there are no limits fixed by nature. Houses
are simply a matter of supply and demand." And that the
London building system is not so unfair or confiscatory
a thing as Mr. Harrison would have us believe is shown
not only by the enormous fortunes which many of the
chief London builders are known to have made, but also by
the fact that shrewd men of business like Mr. Harrison himself are in the habit of investing largely in leasehold houses.

IV.

ASSUMING for the moment that some measure of Leasehold Enfranchisement is desirable in the interests of the public, we may next proceed to inquire whether Mr. Lawson's Bill would do substantial justice as between lessors and lessees. In the first place, then, with regard to the length of term which should qualify a lessee for Enfranchisement, some of the strongest supporters of the principle of Leasehold Enfranchisement think twenty years an unduly short term. Mr. Simpson, indeed, would limit Enfranchisement to cases in which there were something like fifty or sixty years of the lease to run; and Mr. Harrison said that, except in the case of a lease at a rack-rent or an improved ground-rent, he thought twenty years too short, because the reversion was then come within such a measurable and calculable distance of the end that it had ceased to be a matter of actuarial value. Against the opinions of these two lawyers, however, it is only fair to set the judgment of Mr. Parry, an estate agent and accountant at Bethesda, who said he would give yearly tenants the power to enfranchise, and even declared himself "in favour of compelling all landlords to sell their rights in all the cottages to everybody;" and of Mr. Holmes, the Oddfellow and Forester, who maintained that every tenant and every occupier ought to have the right to acquire the freehold of the house he inhabited. But these extreme views must be regarded merely as pious opinions which have not yet been officially sanctioned by the Enfranchisement Association.

As to the provision for the costs of Enfranchisement—of which, as we have seen, only one set is to be allowed as payable by the lessee, except in cases where the court shall otherwise decide—Mr. Gregory, a solicitor of very great experience and a member of Parliament for many years, showed in his evidence how unfairly such a provision would work. The chairman, Mr. Fry, having pointed out what the clause in question said on the subject, Mr. Gregory professed his inability to understand it. "Supposing," said he, "you have to deal with four parties, as I say, you have to deal with the owner of the reversion, you have to deal with the lessee for ninety-nine years, you have to deal with the mortgagee of the owner, and you have to deal with the mortgagee of the lessee for ninety-nine years; that is four different parties to deal with. Are you only to pay one set of costs, to be divided amongst those four parties?" "That is the intention of the Bill," replied Mr. Lawson complacently; "the Bill was drafted by Mr. Broadhurst, and that was Mr. Broadhurst's intention, I think." "I can hardly fancy the Legislature sanctioning that," said Mr. Gregory. "It does then come back exactly to what I say, that you are making parties pay for having their property taken away from them against their consent." And Mr. Josiah Thomas, who is by no means opposed to the general principle of Enfranchisement, in the evidence which he gave last April said he thought the costs should not be limited; the man who put the machinery of the law in motion for the purpose of acquiring the fee should have to pay fair taxed costs.

The absence of reciprocity is another point on which a good deal might be said. In the case of copyhold enfranchisement, of course, either the lord or the tenant can compel the other to enfranchise; but no similar provision is contemplated here. Mr. Harrison, indeed, said that he personally saw no objection to the insertion of a power enabling a landlord to buy up his tenant's interest compulsorily, though he would not give a landlord the right to compel his tenant to buy the reversion. And Mr. Parry said the same power that was given to the lessee he would also give to the landlord, and he would not object to being himself bought out by Lord Penrhyn upon a proper valuation of the property. But, as the chairman suggested, some little difficulty might arise if both parties wished to buy, and there can be no doubt that the rank and file of the Enfranchisers would be highly indignant at the insertion of any such mutual provision. What is sauce for the goose is not, in their opinion, sauce for the gander.*

Another obvious objection to Mr. Lawson's Bill is that under it a landowner would get no compensation for compulsory sale nor for severance. On both these points the Bill differs from the Lands Clauses Act, although a railway company is never empowered to take land compulsorily unless it has been proved that such taking will be for the benefit, not merely of the company itself, but of the public generally, and although the value of the remaining property of the landowner is often enormously enhanced by the railway. Severance of a landowner's estate by carving out of it a number of detached freeholds could not under any circumstances enhance its value, and, as many of the witnesses before the Committee said, might greatly lessen its value.

---

* Many of the Enfranchisers seem, indeed, to have little sense of fair play or justice and no notion what a bargain means. Thus at one of the Association's annual meetings Mr. Broadhurst complained bitterly that although his house was then worth ten or twelve pounds less than it had been worth some years before, the ground-rent on it remained the same. "This," said he, "is a monstrous inequality, which ought to be rectified as soon as possible." And Mr. Hughes, of Holyhead, after telling the Committee that at a certain date many houses in the place had become vacant, was asked if the ground-rent had been remitted in the case of those houses. "It did not," as Mr. Lawson put it, "make any difference to those landowners whether the town was developing steadily or whether there was a retrogression." It would be interesting to know whether, in the opinion of Messrs. Broadhurst and Lawson, the lessee of a considerable area which has lately reverted to Lord Cadogan and for which his lordship is said to have hitherto received an annual ground-rent of five pounds ought to have had his ground-rent increased from time to time as the property rose in value.

Another and perhaps a still more vital and essential defect in Mr. Lawson's Bill, so far as fairness to the lessor is concerned, lies in the fact that the option of purchase which it proposes to confer upon lessees is to be unlimited in point of time. Mr. Cooper, of Beckenham, gave some remarkable evidence on this head. It appeared that he himself, as a builder, often gave his tenants a right to purchase their leases at any time during the first two or three years of their terms ; but if he were to give them a right to purchase during the whole of their fourteen or twenty-one years' leases, it would prevent him from selling the property to any one else. " I think," he said, " it would be detrimental " to have such a power on a tenant's part hanging over one's head throughout the lease. And being asked why he thought that such a right ought to be given to him as against his landlord, he answered frankly enough, " I admit I came here with selfish motives." Mr. Gregory put the point very plainly : " All the lessors that I have been concerned for, or that I have known, would decidedly have objected to a provision that enabled the other party to purchase at any time the property which was leased to him. You see what you are doing ; you are giving him the opportunity at any period for ninety-nine years "— seventy-nine rather—" that he chooses to select to buy out your freehold. It may be that money at one time is more favourable than it is at another, and that he can raise money at a cheaper rate ; he would take advantage of that ; buy at that time ; and then you must invest at a low rate of interest if you are to receive the money. Therefore it is clearly importing into the contract a condition, as I say, to the disadvantage of one party to the existing contract."

Consequent upon this unlimited option to purchase, a general depreciation in ground-rents would inevitably ensue. "No one," said Mr. Mathews, " would buy ground-rents if he were subject to the possibility of their being taken from him, and not only of their being taken from him, but of his having to go into court to discuss their value." And Mr. Martin said that a man would not be able readily to sell his ground-rent subject to the option. "People who buy ground-rents buy for permanent investment; the process of buying costs something in the way of law, and they do not buy with the idea of having, perhaps, the next week to sell again." A lessee would thus be doubly favoured; for the same measure which enabled him to force his landlord to sell would insure his being able to buy on exceptionally easy terms.

There are several other points—some of them brought out in Mr. Mathews's evidence—on which the equity and justice of this Bill, as between lessee and reversioner, might without difficulty be impugned. But inasmuch as Colonel Hughes, the member for Woolwich, seems almost to have admitted that had his own abortive Enfranchisement Bill been quite fair it would have been quite unworkable, it is unnecessary and useless to discuss the subject further.

V.

HAVING thus seen that Mr. Lawson's Bill is not only grounded on unjust charges, but is in itself unjust, we must now go on to inquire whether it or some other measure of Leasehold Enfranchisement is not, after all, a necessity of the times. For of course things do occasionally come to such a pass that it is impossible to carry out some reform which is absolutely essential in the general interest without inflicting grievous hardship or injury on some particular class of people. And this may very well be the case with this question of enfranchising leaseholds, if the London

building-lease system is (as Mr. Lawson says it is) the real
and true cause of much that disturbs and hampers trade
and vitiates the life of the industrial classes of the metropolis. What, then, would be the results of Leasehold Enfranchisement, which the Royal Commissioners seemed to
think might conduce greatly to the improvement of the
dwellings of the people of this country? Whom would it
benefit, and whom would it injure?

Mr. Rhodes, who appears to have represented the
Leaseholds Enfranchisement Association, ld the Committee
that in advocating Leasehold Enfranchisement he really
had in view the thousands of occupying leaseholders who
exist throughout England. It can hardly, however, be pre-
tended that any measure of this kind would primarily relieve
or benefit occupiers. In a fashionable suburb like Becken
ham, where Mr. Rhodes resides, the proportion of persons
who might be affected by such a measure would of course
be exceptionally large ; but it needs no expert evidence to
prove—what, indeed, is the commonest of common knowledge—that the vast majority of occupiers hold and will
continue to hold on terms of less than twenty years. In
fact, Mr. Rhodes himself stated that if any one thought the
whole scheme of Leasehold Enfranchisement was to enable
the tenant to become his own freeholder, nothing that the
Association had put forward would warrant such an idea.
And Mr. Johnson, the town clerk of Nottingham, an entirely
disinterested witness, told the Committee that the tenants,
the working men of Nottingham, were the last people there
who could benefit by the Bill.

That the working men themselves have begun to realise
this is shown by many articles and letters which have been
published from time to time in some of the more advanced
Radical newspapers. Thus, a correspondent of the *Weekly
Dispatch*, who signed himself " A Workman," advocating a
year ago the return to Parliament of men like a certain

gentleman named R. Whitmore, wrote as follows :—" Here is a man who knows something of the condition of the working classes and their needs. . . . He knows where 'the shoe pinches.' If the Liberals and Radicals who want our votes knew it as well, and acted accordingly, there would not be so much political apathy among the workmen of this metropolis. Leaseholds Enfranchisement has no charms for us." The *Financial Reformer* of last July expressed the opinion that " Leasehold Enfranchisement will not break the land monopoly. It may increase the number of landlords, but what is wanted is something that will break the power of landlordism." The *Star*, while admitting that "up to a point the Leasehold Enfranchisement agitation has been a very good thing," because " it has stirred the festering mud of the landlord and tenant system " and "has helped to awaken the capitalist middle-class man," says that there is not much more to be said for the movement and a good deal to be said against it. *Justice*, the organ of the Social Revolution, naturally regards the whole agitation as a mere fraud. " If Mr. Broadhurst," writes the editor, "ever imagined that his Bill would be of any service to the working classes, the avidity with which large property owners seized and utilised the idea should have quickly undeceived him. As a matter of fact, the measure is entirely middle-class and reactionary. . . . Experience teaches us that the small property owner is the worst landlord, and the subletter the most harsh in exacting his rent. To compel freeholders to sell to leaseholders on the demand of the latter is to give encouragement to one of the most grinding classes in the community." On the other hand the *St. Stephen's Review*, which is understood to be the mouthpiece of the Tory Democracy, says that " the Enfranchisement of Leases, with compulsory sale at Government valuations, is sure to become law. It is no party question ; but the Radicals intend to make it so. It is one of the planks of

c

their platform. It ought to come from the Conservative side. Will not Lord Randolph Churchill adopt it, and devote his powerful advocacy to protecting the people against landlord rapacity? . . . The accumulation of wealth beyond the wildest dreams cannot go on, and the Conservative party should grapple with the question, and earn the undying gratitude of an oppressed people. This is no revolutionary proposal."

Whether it was a revolutionary proposal or not, and whether the *St. Stephen's Review* was right or wrong in prophesying that Leasehold Enfranchisement will become law, there can be no doubt whatever that the people chiefly to be benefited by such a law would be not the occupiers, nor the rack-rented tradesmen whose " good-will " is said to be so often " confiscated " by their unscrupulous landlords, but the much-abused lessees or middlemen. Even at Woolwich, where the working men regularly employed at the Arsenal are said to hunger after freeholds, Colonel Hughes himself admitted that in respect of three-fourths of the houses working men would derive no advantage from his Bill. This, however, he said, was only what he intended. " The man who built the house, or who purchased the house, is the man I intend to get the benefit. He may be called ' builder,' or he may be called ' middleman,' but it is the man who puts his property upon another man's land that I want to be able to enfranchise." Mr. Josiah Thomas said that " the man who holds the rent, whom we call the rack-rent landlord, is the man who would enfranchise." And Mr. Farrant, the Managing Director of the Artizans, Labourers, and General Dwellings Company, being asked who would benefit by Leasehold Enfranchisement, answered, " I think middlemen, who are largely interested in promoting to a considerable extent the movement for Leasehold Enfranchisement." And he added that the scheme had been promoted chiefly by these people for the benefit of themselves, and not for the benefit of the working classes, and that he knew a great many men who took a very active part in promoting Enfranchisement, and their favourite mode of investment was to get ground leases from large landlords, and improve the property and get very high rentals. He had heard some of them boast of getting ten and even twelve per cent. They were members. of the Leaseholds Enfranchisement Association. A smaller but more deserving class of persons likely to be benefited by Leasehold Enfranchisement was pointed out by Mr. Tewson, who said it would be an excellent thing for surveyors. "I believe that if you were to pass this Bill I should make a fortune, while I shall now go on slaving to the end of my days. I should want no other business if this Bill were carried." And Mr. Sargant, in his book on "Ground-Rents and Building Leases," remarks that "the effect of the passing of any effective measure of Leasehold Enfranchisement would be to increase the mass of conveyancing done by professional men. This increase would be most considerable during the first few years after the passing of any Act, but would, to a lesser extent, probably be permanent, inasmuch as the length and difficulty of a freehold title are, as a rule, greater under the present law than those of a leasehold title." Beyond these three classes of persons—middlemen, surveyors, and conveyancers—and a sprinkling of occupying lessees, Leasehold Enfranchisement would apparently benefit nobody.

VI.

ON the other hand, divers and numerous classes of persons can be named upon whom any scheme of Leasehold Enfranchisement would inflict grievous and irreparable injury. That the great landowners in London and other large towns would be seriously prejudiced by such a measure goes of course without saying. Their estates would be taken from them bit by bit, they would receive inadequate compensation for the bits taken, and only the deteriorating bits would be left on their hands. This arrangement will perhaps appear hardly fair to men who agree with Mr. Balfour that " even the rich are God's creatures and deserve the protection of the law." It must be admitted, however, that the average British elector cannot easily work himself or be worked by others up to a high pitch of enthusiasm in the cause of the very rich. Come what may, he is wont to argue, these millionaires will always have enough to live on. But even the average British elector might well fight shy of a movement which, as he must perceive plainly enough, could never be confined to an attack upon millionaires. For it is the greatest mistake in the world to imagine that this contest lies entirely or mainly between the great landowners on the one side and the masses of the people on the other side. The masses of the people, as we have already seen, are not primarily or immediately interested in the issue ; and that Leasehold Enfranchisement would hit hard a large number of persons who are not and never will become great landowners is about as certain as anything can-be. Several of the witnesses called before the Town Holdings Committee gave evidence on this point. Mr. Mathews said he himself was a trustee for three children who had lost their parents. " The settled property in respect of which they are beneficiaries is a small building estate. It is let on twenty-five leases at ground-rents amounting in the aggregate to £154, or an average of £6 per lease. The shortest term has about forty years to run. Under a system of compulsory Enfranchisement the trustees might be obliged to appear before some tribunal in twenty-five inquiries, for the purpose of assessing the value of the ground-rent and reversion, and with no funds at their disposal to defend the interests of the beneficiaries. Then if they were bought out, and the cash paid, the trustees would have to pay the costs upon every re-investment of the purchase-money. There are a vast number of similar cases." And Mr. Statter said : "There is no class of security, in my opinion, that was by trustees and others so much sought after as well-secured ground-rents ; " but he added that since this question has been agitated ground-rents in and around Manchester which used to realise twenty-five years' purchase without any difficulty are now selling for about twenty-two years' purchase. We all know, moreover, that in these days of low interest it is practically impossible for trustees to find any other four per cent. investment, so that the income of a trust fund which had been invested in freehold ground-rents would on Enfranchisement be considerably reduced.

Charitable and other public trusts would, of course, suffer equally with private trusts, and the mischief in their case would be far more conspicuous and widespread. Mr. Bourne, the Duke of Bedford's London agent, referred in his evidence to the case of the Harper Charity, which has its property in London but its well-known school at Bedford. This school, said Mr. Bourne, "has an average income of about £20,000 a year from London property, chiefly from ground-rents, or what we may call repairing rents. The whole scheme of education there is based upon that income. The scholarships are fixed upon it ; the masterships, and all the educational advantages, are

based upon having that income. Now what is the result?
I have no hesitation in saying that if this compulsory
Leasehold Enfranchisement scheme ever became law; if
ever such a catastrophe as that arrived, this would happen
to the charity : that instead of having, first of all, their
regular income of £20,000 a year, it would begin to
fluctuate from the very first year of the passing of the law,
and gradually, and probably in the course of five or ten
years, or whatever it might be, that income would drop
down from £20,000 to £15,000. The whole of the
charity would be disorganised ; the scholarships would
disappear ; the masterships would have to be reduced ; the
whole scheme of education that is carried on at that public
school would have to be changed; and simply for what?
Not for the benefit of the community; the community
would be harmed by it ; but for the benefit of some two or
three or four hundred lessees in London, who would put
that additional £5,000 into their pockets, instead of its
going into the pockets of the charity." And Mr. Mathews
calculated that King Edward's School, Birmingham, with
which he has been connected for twenty-five years, and
which has a present rental of about £30,000 a year, would
lose about £9,000 a year if Leasehold Enfranchisement
were carried. " I believe," he said, " that the whole of the
future educational culture of Birmingham depends upon
the preservation of the real property of King Edward's
School." Three other Birmingham charities—the Mason
Science College, the Mason Orphanage, and Lench's Trust
—would all, he said, be affected in a similar way, though
not to so great an extent as the free school : so would
several of the Oxford colleges and some of the London
hospitals. The future usefulness of all these institutions
would be very largely curtailed by Leasehold Enfranchisement.

And, apart altogether from public or private trusts, a

great many thrifty and provident but not particularly wealthy people have been accustomed to invest in well-secured ground-rents, and these persons would suffer at least as much as the Dukes from the proposed legislation. Speaking of the investors in ground-rents Mr. Gregory said : " They are people of all classes, and I may say generally that the investors in these ground-rents are a very meritorious class. They forego large interest during the current lease. They invest in these ground-rents as provisions for their families. A gentleman came to me the other day, one of my old constituents, a tradesman of Brighton, who had a good deal of property. He had been a prudent man, and he said, I do not know what is to come to us ; I have been foregoing my income for the purpose of making provision for my family, and I have done it by means of these ground-rents. I have looked to the reversion ; is that to be taken away from us ? He had been a very Liberal politician too." And Mr. Tewson mentioned a case of his own which had occurred seven or eight years before. " I bought freehold ground-rents of £36 a year for my own investment, for which I gave £5,000. They had nearly thirty years to run, and I am satisfied for the thirty years to receive something less than three-quarters per cent. for my money, knowing that that property is coming into reversion and will benefit my family after me ; and that is the case with scores and hundreds of investors in like manner." Yet the Leasehold Enfranchisers, who would put a stop to this sort of thing, have the assurance to pretend that their scheme is designed to encourage thrift.

Another class of people who would be injured and even ruined by Leasehold Enfranchisement are the small builders possessing little or no capital. These men, as Mr. Garrard said, " would be entirely swept out if they were obliged to buy the fee simple." If builders were prevented from taking the land on an annual payment, Mr. Josiah Thomas said,

" it would stop the building altogether." Even Mr. Cooper admitted that it "would tend to stop the building business." And Mr. Edward St. Aubyn, Lord St. Levan's brother and agent, gave an excellent illustration of this tendency. Lord St. Levan, he said, has decided to sell the existing leases on his estate where the lessees will buy, and to offer the land on freehold tenure. A practical difficulty has arisen, however, because the builders, as a rule, ask for and prefer to build on leasehold tenure. " I can give many examples," said Mr. St. Aubyn, " but one in particular occurs to me with regard to one of the principal builders. He recently offered to build six of the best class of villas, costing at least £2,000 each, but he told me that he would have nothing to do with the scheme if he had to purchase the freehold. He is now erecting the houses on terms which he has accepted for leasehold tenure." Nor would the small builders be the only people to come to grief. As everybody knows,

> When merchants break, o'erthrown
> Like nine-pins, they strike others down.

And it is manifest that the ruin of these builders would mean the ruin of thousands of men whom they employ or who supply them with materials, and that the general public—especially the poorer classes—would suffer considerably from the increase in the rents which the decrease in the supply of houses would infallibly produce.

This, moreover, is not the only or the most direct way in which Leasehold Enfranchisement would injure the working classes. Representatives of the three principal London Companies for supplying artizans' dwellings expressed an unanimous opinion that on freehold land in the centre of London it is impossible to build working men's houses which will pay ; and Mr. Mathews said that "you cannot erect artizans' dwellings on any land which is worth more than 1s. a yard." But what cannot be done on a purely commercial basis, and what the poorer ratepayers naturally do not like to see done by means of the rates, "the bloated ground landlords of London" have in many cases done at their own cost. For instance, Mr. Farrant said that his Company (the Artizans, Labourers, and General Dwellings Company) had taken from Lord Portman, on lease for ninety years, about an acre of land at Lisson Grove, at a ground-rent of 2d. a superficial foot, the market value of the land for other purposes being about 6d. a foot. They proposed to spend about £40,000 on the buildings, and to provide about 700 living rooms ; and they expected to be able to let the rooms at an average of 2s. 3d. a room. Such rents would be impossible if the market price were paid for the land, and if it belonged to a number of freeholders there would be no chance of getting the land for less than the market price. "There is no hope at all," said Mr. Farrant, "for building artizans' dwellings at popular prices except through the great landlords." Mr. Gatliff, the Secretary of the Metropolitan Association for Improving the Dwellings of the Industrious Classes, agreed that the thing cannot be done on strict commercial principles. Mr. Moore, the Secretary of the Improved Industrial Dwellings Company, said that in his opinion the effect of a system of Leasehold Enfranchisement on a Company like his would be that they would be wholly unable to obtain sites for the erection of working-class dwellings ; for they would have to pay the small owners the full value of their interests, and that value would no doubt be prohibitive. With reference to nine blocks of dwellings which his Company were then erecting on the Duke of Westminster's land near Oxford Street, and which would accommodate about 2,000 people, Mr. Moore said that if the Company had had to deal with a large number of separate owners it would have been utterly impossible to carry out any such scheme without statutory powers, and statutory powers would have

c *

made it so expensive that they could not possibly have
done it.   And it must not be supposed that this active and
self-sacrificing interest in the housing of the working classes
is confined to the great landowners of London.   Mr.
Statter, the agent for Lord Derby's Bury estate, said that
his lordship had for many years refused to allow an artizan's
house to be built on less than about 125 square yards of
land, and that this regulation had been subsequently
adopted by the authorities of the town, their by-laws being
drawn on the principle that a given quantity of land should
be devoted to each house.   And Mr. St. Aubyn mentioned
a case at Devonport in which Lord St. Levan, with the
help of the compulsory powers possessed by the Corporation of the town, had carried out a scheme for the erection
of artizans' dwellings at a cost to himself of £8,000 and a
saving to the ratepayers of £20,000.   The site, which he
had let at exceptionally low ground-rents, was a large area
of four or five acres, and the houses accommodated over
1,000 people.

That ratepayers in general must be injured by any
measure which would prevent the execution of public improvements, or would throw the cost of them upon the rates, little
evidence is required to prove.   Yet there can be no doubt
that improvement schemes, which cost the ratepayers such
enormous sums when they are carried out by public bodies
armed with compulsory powers, are frequently carried out
by individual or corporate landowners at their own expense.
"When a ninety-nine years' lease falls in," said Mr. Garrard, "there is a great advantage to all concerned in carrying
out improvements by re-arranging the streets and rebuilding
houses that are, at the present moment, unsuited to the
district."   And he mentioned an instance which had occurred
within his own experience in the neighbourhood of the

City-road. The property in question comprised about 750 cottages, many private houses, and some business premises. "The greater number of the cottages were worn out and unhealthy, upwards of 600 were removed, the streets widened and improved, and healthy dwellings erected to accommodate as many persons as were residing on the property before their removal." And Mr. Statter said that if a measure for compulsory Leasehold Enfranchisement were passed, "legislation must necessarily take place to enable the authorities of the various towns to possess themselves of such properties as would be requisite for the improvement of the towns. They are not called upon to pay for this as far as Bury is concerned, because we"—Lord Derby's representatives—"attempt to promote the interests of the town of Bury by sacrificing these properties instead of calling upon the ratepayers to pay for them." Of course, as he explained subsequently, "the more the town of Bury or any other town improves, the better it is for the owners of property. What I meant to say was this: that instead of compelling the town to spend their money and the money of the ratepayers in doing these things, he throws down the property himself, opens the new streets and roads and arterial communications, instead of compelling the authorities of the place to buy it at the expense or the ratepayers." The real force of the argument lies in this very fact that we have not to appeal merely to the generosity or public spirit of the great landowners, but that, as the late Mr. Edward Bailey, one of the trustees of the Portland Marylebone estate, put it, in such matters "a liberal policy in the long run is a wise policy." "It was a considerable benefit to the town, and a benefit or course to the property," said Mr. Mathews of an improvement which he effected a few years ago on some land belonging to King Edward's School, Birmingham. This land was three or four acres in extent, and he had "cleared the entire site, cut a new street across it, and widened and improved the existing one." This improvement could not possibly have been carried out had several of the houses been enfranchised, and it certainly would not have been carried out by the Town Council. A similar improvement on the London Estate of Rugby School, in "a very insanitary slum known as Little Ormond-yard," was mentioned by Mr. Martin in his evidence.

Not only individual or corporate landowners acting primarily in their own interests, but municipal Corporations acting solely for the benefit of the inhabitants of their several towns, would be seriously hampered and prejudiced by any measure of Leasehold Enfranchisement. Mr. Johnson said that at Nottingham the system of ninety-nine years' leases oftentimes enabled the Corporation to carry out public improvements when the leases fell in. "I have an instance before me now," he said, "where leases fell in. We prescribed a new building line, and compelled a certain class of property to be erected there, and so improved the street. We have done it in several instances." "We are waiting now," he added, "for a lease to fall in in about seven years of two very long streets —Canal-street and another street—and then we shall make a very large town improvement as soon as those leases fall in. That town improvement would have had to be carried out under a Provisional Order, the land taken compulsorily under the Lands Clauses Consolidation Acts, and would have cost us such a sum of money that we should not have presumed to touch it." And he said that the feeling in the Corporation was quite against Parliament enfranchising corporate property, "especially in view of the fact that we should hand down greatly reduced rentals to our successors. If over twenty-five years ago, for instance, our estate had been sold and turned into Consols, we should have a less income from our estate. Instead of that we have three times the income we then had from it, because

we are gaining for the good of the community all the increased value of the estate." Leasehold Enfranchisement,
he maintained, "would be a very grave injustice to us as a
corporation. We should be burdened with the Freeman's
Estate, for instance, to the amount of twopence or three-
pence in the £ in the rates, instead of receiving £40,000
or £50,000 from it ; instead of receiving that sum, it
would be gone." Mr. Mathews said that the Town
Council of Birmingham had expended a million and a
half in purchasing a freehold site in the centre of the town,
and had made a very important street through it. A large
portion of the site they had let upon leases for seventy-five
years. If the Town Council were to be compelled to sell
it all to different lessees, "of course it would entirely destroy
the future financial success of the scheme, the properties
being acquired for the purpose of rendering the Town
Council landowners (at least, that is one of the effects of
the proceeding), and of getting the advantage of the ulti-
mate increment of value." And Mr. Forwood, who has
propounded a scheme whereby the Corporation of Liverpool would fifty-three years hence come into a property
worth twelve millions and a half and all the rates of the
city would thereupon cease, said that if a Leasehold Enfranchisement Act were passed their property would practically "disappear and fritter away." "I am," he said,
"strongly an advocate of the Corporation owning property.
I see advantages from it in the past and would like to continue it. . . . The Enfranchisement of leaseholds is for the
benefit of the leaseholders who are there, and to the detri-
ment of thousands of the poorer ratepayers, to whom the
rates are of very serious consequence."

VII.

IT would be easy to enumerate several other classes of
people whom this or any scheme of Leasehold Enfranchisement must necessarily injure, but perhaps enough has
already been said to show that the inevitable evils which
would result from such a measure are infinitely greater than
any advantages which could possibly be claimed for it.
Let it not be supposed, however, that the Enfranchisers
have little or nothing to say for themselves.   On the
contrary, they have a wonderful collection of arguments and
assertions adapted for use on every emergency and calculated to conciliate every kind of audience.   Readers of
Pope's letters will remember one of them in which he
said that everybody valued him, but everybody for a
different reason : one for his adherence to the Catholic
faith, another for his neglect of Popish superstition ; one
for his good behaviour, another for his whimsicalities ; Mr.
Titcomb for his pretty atheistical jests, Mr. Caryll for
his moral and Christian sentences ; Mrs. Teresa for his
reflections on Mrs. Patty, Mrs. Patty for his reflections
on Mrs. Teresa.   In much the same way the cause of
Leasehold Enfranchisement is made to appeal to all
sorts and conditions of men for all sorts of inconsistent
reasons.   Addressing a Tory Democratic audience, Messrs.
Broadhurst and Reid can expose the iniquities of house
farmers and lament "the want of control by landowners
who have granted long leases ; " or, passing on to an
assemblage of Radical working men, they can denounce
a system which "confers upon landlords a degree of
authority and a right of interference in regard to the
homes of the people which is unendurable in a free
country." Mr. James Platt, who has written treatises on most
subjects and has made a great number of reckless state-

ments on the subject of landlords and tenants, can summon
the reformer to do battle with " this unjust system, the relic
of a defunct feudalism, when men were serfs "; the *Daily
News* can with equal ease arouse our indignation at a
mushroom growth of which the first living authority on
the subject cannot find a single instance earlier than the
year 1783. The travelled cosmopolitan is reminded that,
though building-leases are well known in Paris, they have
no existence in Spain or Servia, in Roumania or in Russia ;
while the insular, old-fashioned Briton is urged to shake off
the trammels of a system which, as an American gentleman
said at the recent meeting of the British Association, is
developing insidiously in the United States, and which, we
suppose, is for that very reason unfit for the loyal subjects
of Queen Victoria.

Moreover, if consistent arguments and definite facts fail
them, the Enfranchisers always have prejudice and sentiment to fall back upon ; and sentiment and prejudice will
carry people a tolerably long distance nowadays. The
philanthropists and the middlemen—the persons who sign
Supplementary Reports and the persons who, as Mr. Tewson
says, " are running about now hoping that they may be
enabled to make fortunes if this Bill passes "—are wont to
point to the poverty, the squalor, the vice, and the crime
which abound in every great city, and, with conscious or
unconscious ingenuity, to connect them with the practice of
building houses on the leasehold system. Occupying lessees
are, of course, only too glad to hear that the salvation of the
country depends on the passing of a Bill which will in all
probability take money out of other people's pockets and
put it into theirs. Amiable enthusiasts, who have never
learned or have forgotten

> How small, of all that human hearts endure,
> That part which laws or kings can cause or cure,

and who are inclined to regard the State and the statute-book as the universal remedy for the ills of life, naturally join in an agitation which promises to confer innumerable benefits on mankind. If ever it occurs to any one of them to question the justice or the expediency of so violent and wholesale an upsetting of contracts as Leasehold Enfranchisement would involve, his doubts are at once removed by some vague but well-sounding cant about "public policy." "We base our demand," says Mr. Howard Evans, "upon the simple proposition that the terminable leasehold system is contrary to public policy. Everything turns upon that. If we cannot prove it, we have no case ; if we do prove it, our case is impregnable." Be it so. The believers in *laisser-faire* will be quite content to meet Mr. Evans on that ground. Only let him bear in mind that, as Sir George Jessel said in one of his remarkable judgments, "if there is one thing more than another which public policy requires, it is that men of full age and competent understanding shall have the utmost liberty of contracting. . . . You have this paramount public policy to consider—that you are not lightly to interfere with this freedom of contract."

Much of the strength of the Enfranchisement agitation springs, no doubt, from sentimental ideas associated with freeholds and freeholders. In our day, as in the Psalmist's, imaginative people like to think that their houses shall continue for ever and that their dwelling-places shall endure from one generation to another. Mr. Evans says "there is something sacred in a house which is the permanent memorial of the father's or grandfather's thought and self-denial." "To sell the old home, which the son or grandson saw the old man buying shilling by shilling, would be almost an act of filial impiety." If this be so, filial impiety must be terribly on the increase at the present time. It has been deliberately encouraged by the Legislature, and in truth it often seems difficult to avoid it—particularly in cases where the son or grandson has to share the old man's savings with a number of inconvenient brothers and sisters. Perhaps, however, Mr. Evans is imbued with the ancient freehold notions respecting the rights of primogeniture. Be that as it may, most of this tall talk about the family house which descends from father to son through countless generations has an uncommonly hollow ring about it at this time of day. Look at the freehold cities and towns of England. What percentage of houses there remain in the same families for ninety-nine years? What percentage of families remain in the same place during that period?

One great difficulty in dealing with these Enfranchisers is that you never know how far they really think and mean what they say. " My dear friend," said Johnson to Boswell, " clear your *mind* of cant. You may *talk* as other people do. But don't *think* foolishly." Mr. Lawson, indeed, must certainly have had his tongue in his cheek when he suggested that the leasehold system was responsible for the depression of trade and for the lives of the industrial classes being vitiated. But Mr. Evans seems to be as serious and as solemn as a judge when he quotes Isaiah and declares in effect that he looks forward to the time when every Englishman shall be his own jerry-builder and his own Gilbey. No arguments, no facts, no evidence will influence men who have arrived at this stage of fanaticism. What Mr. Evans says of the estate lawyers we must be content to say of him and his friends—" We never hoped that these gentlemen would be on our side." But, as Mr. Morley told the House of Commons, though political economy may be in exile, common sense still survives among the bulk of the people of this country. And the more regard they have for common sense, the less attention will they pay to the advocates of Leasehold Enfranchisement.

LONDON:

PRINTED BY CASSELL & COMPANY, LIMITED,

LA BELLE SAUVAGE, E.C.